# LOST IN
# THE MUSEUM

## Miriam Cohen

*Pictures by Lillian Hoban*

A Young Yearling Book

Published by
Dell Publishing
a division of
Bantam Doubleday Dell Publishing Group, Inc.
666 Fifth Avenue
New York, New York 10103

ISBN: 0-440-44780-1

Reprinted by arrangement with Greenwillow Books, a division of William Morrow & Company, Inc.

Printed in the United States of America
November 1983
10 9 8 7 6 5
RAI

For all the Early Childhood teachers
who make school a place Jim likes to be

"This is a big place,"
the teacher told the first grade.
"But if we all stay together,
nobody will get lost in the museum."

Danny said to Jim,
"I know where the dinosaur is.
Come on, I'll show you!"

Jim had never seen a dinosaur.
He ran after Danny.
And Willy and Sammy,
Paul and George did too.

Anna Maria and Sara started after them.
"Come back! You'll get lost!" they called.

Danny slid down the hall very fast.
He slid into a room at the end.
Willy and Sammy, Paul, George, Jim,
Anna Maria and Sara ran after him.

But Jim stopped.
He put his head way back.
He looked up.

Jim heard Willy say,
"That is some big chicken!"
"It's the dinosaur!" shouted Danny.

Jim came around the corner.
The dinosaur had his arms up over
Jim's head. The dinosaur's teeth
were smiling a fierce smile.
Paul said, "Look out, Jim!
He's going to get you!"

Jim turned and ran
as fast as he could.
"Jim, stop!
I was only fooling,"
Paul called.

The kids came running after Jim.
"Don't worry. He won't hurt you,"
said Sammy.
"That's right," Willy told Jim.
"They don't have dinosaurs anymore."

Paul put his arm around Jim.
Anna Maria said, "It's silly to be scared."
Jim knew it was silly.
He wished he could be brave.
"Come on, let's find the others," George said.

"I think we are lost," said Sara.
"I know where to go," Danny said.
They all hurried after him down
the big hall. But there were too
many rooms.

"You got us lost," Anna Maria
said to Danny.
"My toe hurts," said George.
"Maybe we will have to stay here
all night," Paul said.

Jim thought about staying all night
with the dinosaur.
"I will go find the teacher," he said.
"You stay here in case she comes."

Jim went into many rooms.
He kept his eyes shut a little. If he saw
the dinosaur, he could shut them tight.

A big boy was looking at birds' eggs.
Jim said, "Have you seen my teacher?"
Before the big boy could answer,
Jim saw a red coat way down the hall.

Margaret had a red coat! Jim ran to see.
But somebody else was wearing Margaret's coat!

Jim was so tired.
He had to find the teacher!
He had to bring her back to the kids!
He ran on.

Jim saw penguins playing in the snow like first graders. He saw a mother, father, and a child deer. The father stood with one foot in the air.

Jim stopped to rest.
The room was dark.
At first he couldn't see.

Then a great gray whale swam over
his head. He winked at Jim as if
he had something nice to tell him.
Jim looked all the way to the whale's tail.

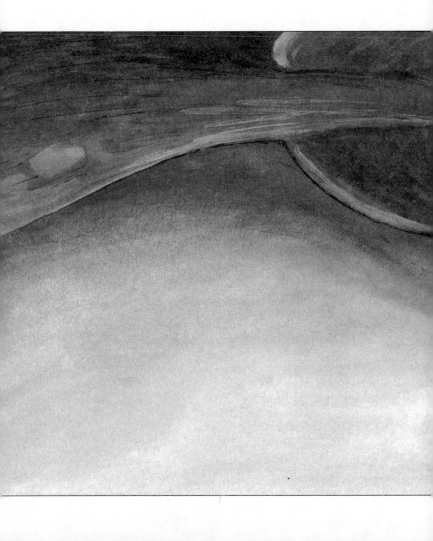

A lady was there with many children.
"Jim!" everybody called. "Oh, Jim!
We have been looking for you."

The teacher said, "Where have you been? Where are the other children?"
"I'll take you there," Jim said.

Jim started back.
He went past the penguins, past the deer
This way? No! That way!
There they were—
George, Willy and Sammy, Anna Maria,
Danny, Paul and Sara.

When they saw their teacher,
George and Sara began to cry.
She hugged them.
"If we had stayed together, this
wouldn't have happened," she said.

Willy and Sammy said, "Jim was brave. He went to find you!"

"Yes," the teacher said, "Jim was very brave. But next time, remember—
IF WE ALL STAY TOGETHER,
NOBODY WILL GET LOST."

They were so glad to be found!
Everybody went to have lunch in the cafeteria
You could choose chicken and dumplings,
crisp fried fish, or beef stew with two vegetable
But they all chose hot dogs.